Approaching Wilderness
Six Stories of Dementia

GENE TWARONITE

Approaching Wilderness
Six Stories of Dementia

Copyright ©2014 by Gene Twaronite
ISBN-13: 978-1502595010
ISBN-10: 150259501X

All rights reserved. No part of this book may be used or reproduced by any means, graphic, electronic, or mechanical, including photocopying, recording, taping or by any other storage retrieval system without written permission from the author, except in the case of brief quotations embodied in critical articles and reviews.

"The Woman Who Came for Lunch" first appeared in *Avatar Review*. "Approaching Wilderness" first appeared in *Forge*. "A Letter of Intent" first appeared in *Sheepshead Review*. "Flash in the Bedpan" first appeared in *The Write Room*. "No Choice" and "Beliefs of My Mother" first appeared in *Wilderness House Literary Review*.

All the characters, names, incidents, organizations, and dialogue in these stories are either the products of the author's imagination or are used fictitiously.

DEDICATION

To Albina

CONTENTS

The Woman Who Came for Lunch	1
No Choice	9
Flash in the Bedpan	13
Beliefs of My Mother	17
A Letter of Intent	28
Approaching Wilderness	37

THE WOMAN WHO CAME FOR LUNCH

"Who is she?" the old man muttered, peeking through the window. "And why is she making a sandwich in *my* kitchen?"

The old man continued to stare as if he had never seen a person make a sandwich before. He watched her delicate hands caressing and alternating the provolone, Swiss, salami, turkey, and deli loaf, and tingled at the thought of being one of the slices. But who is she?

The old man forgot all about the newspaper he had gone to retrieve from behind the hedge. Shivering, he pulled his bathrobe around him. It was just not right. Strange women don't suddenly appear, at least not in his house. Maybe he should call the police and ask them if a missing person had been reported. He felt a headache coming on. Why do these things always happen to me?

****

The old woman tried to concentrate on her sandwich, but she did not like being stared at. Who is he? Maybe he's the gardener. But why was he wearing only slippers and a bathrobe?

She picked up the phone and dialed 9-1-1. "Please help me. There's a man standing outside my window in his bathrobe watching me make a sandwich. What does he look like? Well, he looks kind of sad ... and hungry, too. And he's got really nice gray hair."

Then the old woman gave the dispatcher an address, which was the only one she could remember. It was the house in Brooklyn where she was born.

****

Now she's using my phone. The old man was furious. Who knows, she's probably calling some secret lover in Australia or Japan. He peeked at her again and at the way the late morning sun illuminated the gray streaks in her curly hair. Yes, she would be just the type to have many secret lovers. The thought filled him with sadness. Yet he was also happy for her. A beautiful woman like that deserves to have many lovers.

Still, this did not change anything. There was a strange woman in his kitchen and his feet were getting cold. What should he do?

The Woman Who Came for Lunch

Maybe he should just go inside and find out. It was not his first choice. All his life the old man had tried to avoid direct confrontations. There was usually a safe way around any problem. No sense asking for trouble. Still, it was his house and his food. There was only one thing to do.

****

The old woman looked out the window but the gardener was gone. She decided to call him that after remembering who he reminded her of. It was the handsome, gray-haired gardener who tended the botanical garden that she had visited with her father when she was eight years old. One day, the gardener tipped his hat and bowed, handing her a gardenia. It was the most romantic thing she had ever experienced. Often she would think about him, wishing she could hurry and grow up so she could meet him again.

She sat down at the kitchen table and stared at the sandwich on her plate. She was not hungry now. Eating alone was no fun. Had it always been this way? It didn't seem so long ago that ... what? She struggled to regain some clue to her recent past, but it was no use. Yet she felt there was something or someone important that she should remember. She hated herself. What kind of person would forget such a thing? But why did something she couldn't remember cause her such pain?

****

The old man decided to walk around the block first before confronting the woman. There was nothing in the world, he believed, that couldn't be walked out. He pulled his bathrobe tighter. Maybe he should have changed first. But it was a short block and he was already at the corner of Mayflower Street … The old man stopped and gaped at the street sign. He knew every corner of this neighborhood and there was no Mayflower Street. How could a new street just appear?

Maybe he had somehow gone past the street where he was supposed to turn. The old man spun around and retraced his steps. When in doubt, start from the beginning, he muttered. But the street he had lived on for thirty-six years was nowhere in sight. All the houses seemed out of place. He ran back to the corner to read the sign again—Mayflower and … Hope. That's not my street, he thought. But then, what exactly was it? He tried every memory trick he could think of. But the name had vanished.

He wandered up and down one street after another, searching for some clue that might lead him home. But none of the street names sounded right. With mounting panic, he swept the

The Woman Who Came for Lunch

landscape for some familiar feature, but the harder he looked the more alien it appeared. Nothing made any sense.

The old man started to run, anywhere that might take him away from this nightmare. He was about to give up and ring the nearest doorbell for help when he noticed the house. He was sure he had seen it before. Was he was going in circles? Not a good sign, old boy. Yet there was something more. Perhaps it was the way one of its windows was framed by the evergreen hedges. Or maybe it was the silhouette of a woman eating a sandwich by the window. He knew that woman, but from where? He crept in for a closer look.

****

The old woman ate her sandwich in an unwelcome silence. She strained to hear some comforting sound from the house, something that would tell her things were all right. But all she could hear was her own nasal breathing. She put down her teacup and it made an awful crash on its saucer. It's all wrong.

She began thinking of the gardener again. And she imagined him sitting across from her at the table. He was still wearing his khaki uniform, all worn and green-stained, though his hat was on the rack by the door. She was all grown up now, but he was still the same age as he would always be. He looked into her eyes and planted a gardenia in her hand. The old woman lifted it to her nose and closed her eyes, inhaling deeply. All these years, she had wanted to say so much to him, to tell him all her dreams and private thoughts. But now, she couldn't think of anything to say. And when she opened her eyes, the gardener was gone.

****

The old man slipped quietly through the backdoor and into the hallway. Everything suddenly seemed familiar. Off the hallway to the right he knew was the kitchen. Somehow he had found his way home. He was about to drop to his knees and kiss the floor when he remembered the strange woman in the kitchen. A bead of sweat trickled down his nose as he began to shake. Who is she? Steady, old boy. He gripped the sides of his father's old desk and stared into the hallway mirror.

Then he remembered. It was something he had hidden. Now which drawer was it? Quietly, he pulled open one drawer after another. Each was filled with hundreds of boxes and bottles. He opened several of the containers, only to find smaller and smaller empty containers, apparent decoys for whatever treasures lay concealed there.

The Woman Who Came for Lunch

Where did all these come from? Could someone else be hiding things here? None of the containers seemed familiar. Frustrated, he sat down at the desk. Where was it? Instinctively, he felt behind the black plastic trays inside the desk. Then he found it—a thin cigar box wedged tightly behind the trays. He opened it and gazed upon the objects of his memories: a fossil Trilobite, three packages of colored rubber bands, a golf score card, a headless British tin soldier, two cancelled theater tickets, and a ripped out page from a department store catalog. He held the page reverently. There she was, still as beautiful as ever. Modeling a sleek gown, she was all that a teenage boy could wish for in a woman: beautiful, mature and understanding, someone who would not laugh and who would gladly share his life with him forever. He had been especially taken with the model's pearl necklace and silvery hair and the way she primly crossed her legs in the ad. Suddenly he knew who the strange woman in the kitchen was. He closed the box and placed it back in its hiding place. Then he headed for the kitchen, but not before plucking one gardenia from the garden.

****

Startled, the strange woman turned around as the old man entered. When she saw him standing there framed by the kitchen archway, she smiled as she had not smiled in years. Her gardener was back. He bowed and handed her the gardenia. Stroking her pearl necklace, the woman primly crossed her legs and pulled out a chair.

"Would you like a sandwich?"

NO CHOICE

"We have no choice," her husband told Alice. "When the time comes, someone has to do it for both of us. Don't worry—I'll be quick."

That's what worried her. What if it were so quick that she didn't know it happened? One second she would be here, the next she'd be gone, without a chance to object or say goodbye. She hated the way the thought always overshadowed other things she wished to recall. But now it was all she could think about—that single moment when what little memory was left to her would be obliterated.

She had never actually agreed to it. But her husband was a proud man and couldn't bear the thought of being a burden to anyone. "What happens when I can no longer take care of you, old girl? What will become of us? I don't give a rat's ass what your brother George says. I'm not letting him put us in one of those places. I'd rather die.

They won't take us alive!"

Alice stared at the locked bedroom drawer where her husband had stashed a small rosewood-handled pistol. She had seen it only once, but its image still haunted her. She had always hated guns, and so had her husband. But he had bought it quietly about the same time she had lost the ability to speak except in pitiful grunts.

"What are you staring at, Alice?" as if he didn't know. She smiled, or thought she did—it was so hard to tell—at him sitting in his wheelchair. "Come on, what's wrong?" he asked. So it *wasn't* a smile, after all.

She glanced at the mirror and changed her face. That's better—smile. She didn't want him to get suspicious.

"That's my girl," he said. "We'll get through this, together. There's so little time left, so let's just try to be positive."

What does he mean—"so little time left?" Is he planning on doing it tonight? What if he tries to do it while I'm asleep? Alice glared at her husband.

"What's the matter now?" he asked. I swear, Alice, I can see the way a thought crosses your face. "What are you thinking about?"

I wonder—does he suspect? No, he couldn't. That would be too much for even his powers of perception. I wasn't even sure myself until now.

No Choice

But her husband was right about one thing. There was little time left.

That night, she kept one eye partly open until she knew her husband was fast asleep. She knew his snore cycle by heart and calculated how much time she had. She rose quietly, lingering one last time over the sleeping form of her beloved husband. Despite their many differences, their marriage had survived, and she remembered—or at least chose to remember—more of the good times than the bad. He was a good man who loved her. It was not his fault that he couldn't imagine another reality.

Quietly she unlocked the drawer—her husband was never good at hiding things, including keys to locked drawers—and took out the gun. For a moment she studied it as an artifact whose elegant nickel-plated design belied its primitive function. Yes, it would be a fitting tool with which to kill someone you love. Her mind swirled as she stood over her husband. In the darkness she could just make out the shiny bald head she loved to stroke. He was snoring again. There was little time. Her hands trembled. She must get closer.

She dressed with deliberate calmness, savoring the feel of new garments against her skin. Then she pulled a packed suitcase from the back of the closet. It was a plan she had rehearsed many times, and she was ready, though she could not remember for what. She only knew there was no choice. Looking at her husband, who was no longer snoring now, she closed the bedroom door and slipped into her new life.

FLASH IN THE BEDPAN

Olivia stared at the woman removing the bedpan, then inspected it carefully. Its contents both disgusted and reassured her. It was one of the last links to reality left to her. She smiled at the nurse's aide, thankful for another bowel movement and for still knowing what shit was.

Kara tried to look cheerful. It was not her favorite part of the day, and she couldn't understand why anyone would smile at their shit. But it was her first week and she had much to learn. Gently she helped Olivia upright for a sponge bath.

At first, Olivia coyly resisted as she always did, pulling her arms tightly across her breasts. Then, looking into Kara's eyes, she smiled and relented, opening her arms wide. And as Kara gently washed each part of her body, Olivia began to tense up, then shiver and moan, until at last she gave out an ecstatic cry.

Olivia lay back on her pillow, gazing out the

window with a bemused expression. She had never been an erotic being, of that she was certain. It's not that she hadn't tried, plenty of times. But in the end sex had always left her feeling empty. For a while she had succeeded with the usual tricks in keeping it from her husband, Ernie. Dutifully she would moan and arch her body, often at inappropriate times. A couple of times she even managed to convince herself that she really did feel something. But eventually her husband saw through it and grew increasingly frustrated and resentful of his inability to satisfy her. Three years later, they parted, still good friends, as he went off in search of a more passionate lover.

Though she never remarried, Olivia still hoped to find passion at the touch of another. Before a date she would often practice in the mirror, touching herself tenderly and rehearsing out loud what she might say. But her lovers never bought it and neither did she. And her relationships only led to more resentments and rejections along with a growing sense of futility.

Eventually she stopped going out altogether. She couldn't pretend any more.

But in the classroom it was a different story. In her literature classes she called forth the universe of fictional characters that lived inside her, channeling their words and passions into live performances for her students. She became Emma

Bovary, liberated from a dull life and marriage. Or she became Thomas Hardy's tragic beauty, Eustacia Vye, whose exotic, dark-haired looks Olivia fancied herself sharing. At times the performances seemed more real to her than anything she had ever experienced. In them she found the perfect embodiment of all that she wished to feel.

But she knew too well the lessons from literature. She knew that Eustacia Vye had loved Damon Wildeve only because there was no better object available to her. And to him she was just one more woman to conquer. Olivia had often wondered if she could ever feel Eustacia's one great desire: "To be loved to madness."

"Why does she moan and cry out when I give her a sponge bath?" asked Kara. "Lately she's been repeating a name—Damon or something like that. It's almost as if she's ..."

The charge nurse nodded and smiled. "She's acting out some part of her past. It's common in advanced stages. She's losing speech and all control. She's probably trying to find a place where things still make sense. Just try to go with it."

Later that week, during a sponge bath, Kara noticed that Olivia had become strangely calm and quiet. The tenseness was still there, but it seemed more focused on something inside her. Then Olivia turned to Kara and spoke softly. "Is that you,

Damon? Do you love me now? Tell me; I will know it."

Kara thought quickly, then answered tenderly in a husky voice. "Yes, Eustacia. I do love you. Where do you wish to go? Things will be different now. I promise."

BELIEFS OF MY MOTHER

Abigail couldn't help herself. Every time she looked up from the television, there it was—the dreaded picture gallery on her apartment wall. Why couldn't the staff have put up the pictures someplace else? That way she wouldn't have to look at them every time a commercial came on. Lately it had become like a cemetery filled with the grave markers of strangers. She had begged the attendants to take down the portraits of people she no longer remembered. But they always insisted that the pictures should remain in hopes that they might trigger her memory. Fat chance. She had looked at them hundreds of times to no avail. They were just empty faces—and real dog-faces, some of them. How could any of her relatives or friends be that ugly?

But there was one picture that she did remember. It was a close up of a stout middle-aged woman surrounded by the multi-colored flowers of her garden. The woman's face, though much darker than hers, reminded her of the image she saw each day in the mirror. From the wall her mother smiled back at Abigail across the years, reassuring her that at least some things are forever.

Sometimes Abigail would talk to her mom on the wall. "There you are again, Ma—out in your garden. You do love your flowers. Would you pick a bouquet for me? Maybe some zinnias, delphiniums, and dahlias, and don't forget the sweet williams." And she could imagine her mother's reply. "Well, get off your fat ass, child, and help me pick some!"

Flowers were the one thing about her mother—that and her no nonsense attitude—that Abigail could still remember. But she wished that she remembered other things.

Like what made her mother tick? Abigail knew that her mother loved her, in her tough gentle way. But what did she believe? Was she a Democrat or a Republican, for instance? Abigail thought about that for a while. She couldn't even remember which party she belonged to herself. It would be nice to know that much at least when all those annoying television ads came on, with their babbling heads telling her to vote for them. She didn't give a rat's patootie about any of them.

As another politician appeared on her TV

Beliefs of My Mother

screen, she pointed the remote at the man's smiling face and made him disappear. "Go away!" she shouted. Flipping the channels till she was safely past him, she paused at a show she had often watched with fascination. Here was the same man again in a nice blue suit with a pink carnation in his lapel. He was always shouting about God or crying. This time, he was doing both. And as usual, he was asking for money. People in the audience were cheering and yelling, "I believe! I believe!" The show was on Sundays, because it was always announced with the words "Sunday Morning Worship with the Reverend Thomas B. Fairweather." Was there something special about Sundays that made people believe? All days seemed the same to her.

Did her mother ever watch this show? she wondered. And did she believe in the same God? Abigail struggled to remember any time she had seen her mother watch it. Maybe her God was on a different channel.

Abigail thought about all the other things besides God that people believe in. She remembered a show she had watched yesterday—or was it last year?—on the *History Channel*. It was about the American Revolution. There were a bunch of white guys in funny wigs standing around a table. She didn't remember much of the plot, but the words "all men are created equal" stuck in her head. She thought of her mother. Did she really believe that, she wondered—that black folks were just as good as white folks? And what about women? Abigail's mind raced. She grew slightly dizzy as she always did when too many things popped into her heat at once. Did she believe all that stuff that scientists say about people being related to chimpanzees and how in that show on the *Discovery Channel* everything started with a Big Bang?

But she especially wanted to know if her mother believed in God. And if so, which God? She stared at her mother's smiling face, looking for answers. I know you're in there, Ma. Help me out.

There's nothing in a person's face, Abigail thought, that tells whether a person believes in God, or even if they're a Democrat or a Republican. For all she knew, her mother could have believed in a God like that Hindu elephant deity she had seen on some travel channel— Ganesha or something like that. It was supposed to ride on a mouse and was considered to be the Lord of success. She looked at the dirty old dress her mother wore in the picture. Her mother didn't look very successful, but maybe it was because she didn't pray enough to her elephant God. How exactly are you supposed to pray to an elephant? she wondered. And that poor mouse.

Abigail turned off the TV and stared at the

Beliefs of My Mother

blank screen, trying to recall anything that her mother had ever said or done that had to do with God. But nothing came. She sat back in her rocking chair and gazed at the ceiling. Yes, now she remembered something. It was some kind of solemn occasion. There were flowers everywhere, and her mother was sitting right next to her. This time, she wasn't smiling. There was also a lot of other people all dressed up in black outfits sitting in a dim room. They were looking at a body lying in a long wooden box on a bed of white cushions. Caked with makeup, the dead man's face was as unfamiliar as all the other faces on her wall. Yet there was something about it. Now she remembered. It was the face in the picture next to her mother's. The people in the room were all staring at him, as if waiting for something. They all looked sad and hungry. Then the scene shifted. She was in the kitchen of some house, and the same people were now drinking red wine and eating things from a big table as they made jokes to each other. She saw her mother putting slabs of pink stuff from the table onto her plate and eating them. And for some reason words she had once heard popped into her head: "Whoever eats my flesh and drinks my blood." She shuddered at the thoughts that crowded her mind. What happened to the dead man? Exactly what were they eating? And was that really wine in their glasses or something else? Could her mother have believed in eating people when they died? She shook her head and rocked violently in her chair, moaning softly.

Another scene flashed in her head. This time, she was inside a big white building filled with pews. Pews! Now we're getting somewhere, she thought. What kind of building besides a church has pews? Every row was packed with people dressed up in their Sunday best. Up in front was the silver-haired minister, who was holding a microphone and *singing* along with a five-man blues band and three women backup singers. Everyone was singing joyously, while some even danced in the aisles. And there was her own mother, dancing up a storm like some witchy woman. "Go, Ma, go!" Abigail shouted. "*Hallelujah!*" Then she got up from her chair and danced and shouted till she collapsed on the floor, laughing so hard she peed in her pants.

Abigail cleaned herself off—at least there's one thing she could still manage—and went back to her chair. Still out of breath and laughing, she clutched her heart. Oh my, Abigail. You're not a young girl anymore. And she recalled a time long ago when she was ten, or maybe eleven, marching with her mother in some kind of parade. Only it wasn't the kind of parade where people clap and cheer. Those marching were carrying signs and banners, though she couldn't read or remember what they said. She

Beliefs of My Mother

clung tightly to her mother's hand and to the small sign she carried. People were shouting things—mean, awful things—and there were police holding back vicious dogs. Her mother squeezed her hand, trying to reassure her. There was a grim look on her face, like she was marching into battle with Satan himself.ABigail could see the fear in her eyes. She trembled as she heard once again the sound of the dogs barking and people screaming.

It was a while before Abigail stopped shaking. It was a memory she wished she could erase. She saw her mother, her head bleeding, lying still in the street. "Ma, get up! Please, Ma, don't leave me!" When her mother opened her eyes and slowly rose to her feet, Abigail couldn't stop crying. "It's OK, child," she said, wiping her dress off and putting her hat back on. "*We did it!*"

Exactly what she and her mother did that day she could not remember. But Abigail knew it was important—important enough to die for—which had to mean her mother believed in something. But what if her mother didn't believe in God? Just because she danced in church doesn't prove anything. And if she didn't believe, would that make her a bad person?

Abigail muttered the word softly to herself—"God God God God God God"—gradually increasing the speed of her mantra. Then she shouted it as loud as she could: "*God! God! God!*"

She waited for an echo inside her. She knew what the word meant, and the fact that she was now thinking about God must mean something, but for her it had no connection. Did that mean she didn't believe in God herself, or had she just forgotten how to believe?

She grew tired of thinking about God. She tried thinking about her mother some more. Come on, Abigail, think. Don't give up. Troll your soul. She laughed at the rhyme she had made. She still knew what a soul was, or at least thought she did. It is something inside you that isn't really part of your body, and it has to do with God and heaven and hell. But what did it mean to troll? Wasn't a troll some kind of scary creature? She remembered reading as a child a story that had big hairy trolls in it. What did trolls have to do with anything?

She searched her room, looking for clues. The man in the blue suit was always clutching his bible and quoting verses from it. Yet there were no bibles anywhere. There were no books at all, in fact, for she had stopped reading years ago. Once, she had opened a book down in the lobby while waiting for breakfast. It was some novel that everyone was talking about. All she could see were lines of little black marks running across the pages. Disgusted, she slammed the book shut. But there was a time when she did have books. It was in that other place where she had lived. It was a big yellow house, not this little room. There were books there—all kinds of books—stacked everywhere, even in the garage. But then they all got wet, she remembered, and someone—who was it?—had thrown them all away just because they had gotten all musty. But isn't that the way books are supposed to smell? The memory made her angry. While she couldn't recall any books she had read, she had always felt better having them around. She used to stroke their spines on the shelves, promising herself to read them someday. And then that same person—it was a woman, she now remembered—had bought her a big screen TV, as if that somehow made up for throwing out her books.

Someone knocked at the door. Grumbling, she got up to answer.

"Hi, Mom. Are you having a good day?" It was that same woman again—the one who's always calling her Mom and trying to hug her. Oh no, she's going to do it again—*ugh!*

"OK, Mom, be that way." The middle-aged woman seemed offended, though why Abigail couldn't imagine. That's what you get when you go around hugging strange women. I'm not her Mom. Why can't she accept that? "I'm here to count out your pills. Then I have to run. I've got a big meeting downtown."

Yes, she always had big meetings. Abigail

stared at her quietly as the woman counted the pills. "You sure do have a lot of pills, Mom. Looks like you've got some new ones here. I may have to start charging you overtime." She laughed nervously.

Why did the woman always have to make small talk? Just get on with it. Abigail fidgeted her fingers, waiting for her to finish and get out. Then she remembered who the woman was. It was the same woman who had thrown out her books! How dare she come back here?

"Get out!" cried Abigail. *"Leave me alone!"*

"Oh, Mom, not again. I thought you remembered." Then the woman began to sob.

Abigail began to cry, too. She put her arms around the woman. "There, there, dear—it's all right, I forgive you. And maybe someday you'll find your real mother. And don't forget to close the door on your way out."

Breathing a sigh of relief, Abigail trudged back to her chair and turned the TV back on. Maybe she should look there instead of in her mind. She stared blankly at a commercial, which showed a big green lizard walking in the desert when suddenly a piano fell out of the sky behind him. Is there some meaning in this? she thought. Who is this lizard and what does he want? She shook her head. This is all so complicated. There must be some truth here.

She thought back to all the programs and commercials she had seen on TV, at least those she still could recall. Then she remembered a man's face—a very wise face—and some words that always made her feel good. "And that's the way it is." The way he said it just sounded so right. That's what her mother always said whenever he came on. "Now there's a man you can trust, Abigail—a man you can believe in." But where was the man now? Abigail couldn't remember seeing him lately. She wished he would come on right now and say it again. "And that's the way it is."

Abigail turned off the TV and sat back in her chair, smiling. She didn't want anything to interrupt the memory of that face or voice. It was something to believe in.

A LETTER OF INTENT

George sat at his desk battling his brain. He wished he could punch it. It was not the brain he once knew—always quick with the comeback and able to find the right words. Gradually it had changed, shedding words and abilities under the guise of supposedly normal aging, turning into the alien entity that had taken over his head.

There were tests and more tests, of course, followed by meetings and counseling to determine how much living assistance he would require, and more to the point, whether he had enough money left to afford it. And if he couldn't, there was always the state run nursing home, where old men like him sit and stare while waiting for final release.

But he would not let this half-wit brain win. There was one more thing it must do.

George had weighed his options as carefully as his plaque-clogged cerebrum would permit.

A Letter of Intent

Everyone around him was full of encouraging advice about new treatments and therapies that can delay the worst symptoms for years. They told him to be brave and fight back. Never give up, they chirped. We know how difficult this must be for you.

Yeah, right. They can all go to hell. None of them can possibly know. I wish they would just leave me alone. Let me and my brain disintegrate in peace. But they won't do that, of course, especially not my son-in-law, Frank, who thinks this is some kind of boxing match. Just because he was a middleweight in college, he considers himself an expert on boxing and life in general. "You have to visualize yourself in the ring with this thing. Give it a right jab, then a left. Give it everything you've got. You got to feel it, George. Everything depends on this match. Nobody can fight it but you."

Of course, Frank never won any matches himself. His closest victory was a draw, after his opponent, suffering from the flu, fainted during the first round.

But as with so much of Frank's bullshit, the boxing analogy was all wrong. What George had in mind was more of a writing contest—but one to the death that neither Frank nor George's wife would understand. He thought about Anne, and the story she had told him about when she was five and couldn't stop crying because her pet rabbit had to be put to sleep. For her, ending the rabbit's suffering was simply not enough to accept the monstrous decision to take its life. No, she would never accept it. And she would not forgive him for what he had planned.

George stared at the words he had written in his journal and frowned. Now what was it? Anxiously he flipped back the pages and scanned his words looking for clues. Yes, there it was—the plan. Now he remembered why he had started writing everything down, even the most trivial things. It was his only defense against the alien. And soon, he knew, there would be no more words and their rich connections. There would be only vague thoughts and orphan memories. He must act while there was still time.

Each day the alien was gaining in strength, threatening to destroy what little order was left to him. Often when George looked back at what he had written, instead of the soaring prose he had imagined himself writing, he would find gibberish. There would be whole pages of inane words and phrases like "the hydrocephalous ensemble of vertiginous polymorphs," or even completely made up words such as "tvzzyajjy" and "hyyyyaaapporree!" One of his chief failings as a writer had always been his lackadaisical editing. Ironically, in the past few years he had become a

A Letter of Intent

better editor, detecting and deleting all the crap his brain was now attempting to pass off as prose. His journal was more a patchwork of rational bits, interspersed with crossed out blocks of some madman's ravings.

His goal was to write a perfect letter of his intentions—one that both Anne and others would at least understand, if not accept. It had to be a masterpiece.

So where to begin?

I, George L. Pettingill, being of sound mind...

No, that isn't quite right. His mind isn't sound. But starting with "being of unsound mind" would hardly inspire confidence in his readers. Besides, it's no secret that his cognitive functions are in the toilet. Why dwell on the obvious? Cut to the chase.

When in the course of a human life it becomes necessary for a man to terminate the bonds which hold him to this earth and all that he holds dear, and to achieve a final state of dignity denied him by events beyond his control, a respectful consideration of the feelings and thoughts of others around him requires that he provide a full accounting of the causes that compel him to this separation...

Much better, he thought, but too much like Thomas Jefferson.

The tone needed to be just right—not too formal but not too casual either, lest his readers think he wasn't taking this seriously. He thumbed through his *Letter Writing Handbook*. In the section devoted to formal letters were the following general guidelines: to write as clearly and simply as possible, to make the letter no longer than necessary, and to avoid informal language. Unlike casual letters that bounce all over the place with no set purpose or logic—much like his brain sometimes—formal letters got right to the point. There was a comforting structure to them. There was the salutation, followed by a pithy first paragraph stating the purpose. The middle paragraph, however, contained the real nuts and bolts, setting out all the relevant information behind the writing of the letter. Finally, the last paragraph delivered an ultimatum of sorts, stating what action you expect the recipient to take, which in his case would be to at least accept if not understand his final act.

There were missives for every occasion, ranging from cover letters and letters of intent to birthday invitations and congratulatory notes. George smiled at the last one, recalling the letter of congratulations he had received last Christmas from the CEO of his company.

A Letter of Intent

Dear Mr. Pettingill,

This is to inform you that, based on your many years of exemplary service to Diversified American Family Insurance, the board has unanimously voted to grant you the Outstanding Achievement Award along with a bonus of $50,000.

The amount took his breath away at first, but he was worth it, dammit. However, when he tried to expand upon the memory, George found he couldn't. He shook his head and scowled. Then he remembered. There had never been an award except in his head. Three years ago—or maybe ten—he had written the letter to himself, then posted it. Upon receiving it, he gave in completely to the fantasy, tearing open the letter and poring over its words as if he had never seen them before.

It was just one of the many tricks the alien played on him. But not this time. This letter had to be for real. He was the CEO of his life, and he was stepping down. And here were his reasons. He would write a letter of intent. But to whom should he write it?

To Whom It May Concern:

No, too wishy-washy, he thought. Whoever

picked up the letter could read it as they saw fit, whether it concerned them or not. What did he care when he was gone? There was really only one person he still cared about—only one person to convince.

Dear Anne,

You of all people know what I have been going through, so I hope you'll try to understand what I plan to do. "Till death do us part," we promised, and I intend to keep my end of the bargain, sooner rather than later. By the time you read this, I'll be gone from this world of confusion, or in other words, dead.

I know you have different views on this matter, so I won't try to convince you. At least permit me to explain my reasons for self-termination (which sounds so much less harsh than "killing myself," don't you think?). As you know, Anne, I am a proud man. How often you have reminded me. It will be the death of me, you always said, if I don't learn how to be more humble and accepting of things I cannot change. Well, I can't accept this, and I don't want you or anyone to see me become a zombie while this alien thing I once called a brain takes over. No, Anne, loving creature that you are, even you must not see me like that. I can just see you spoon feeding me, talking to me reassuringly when all I

A Letter of Intent

could hear was pure babble. You would dab the drool from my face, and then cry softly when I stared back at you with an empty look. It is too much to bear. I need to go out while there's still time. I won't go into the details of my departure. Suffice it to say that I have researched all the usual methods, and have found one that is relatively painless and won't mess up the kitchen. I will try to make it look like an accident, though please forgive me if I do not succeed. I have never been good at this sort of thing, and this will be my first and thankfully last time (I hope). And please tell Frank for me that he's an asshole (OK, so you're probably not going to do that).

In conclusion, I will not try to tell you here how many ways I have loved you, for you already know. Of course, you might think my action in leaving you proves otherwise. That is something you must work out for yourself. I can only hope that you will understand and someday forgive me.

Your loving husband, George

George read back what he had written and nodded. Then he painstakingly rewrote it in his best cursive on the linen stationery he had saved for the purpose. He folded the letter and stuffed it into one of the matching envelopes, and filed it away in his desk for later reading. There was still time for one last edit. It had to be perfect.

But the alien had other plans. Later that night, it took the letter out of the desk and addressed it to Anne. Then it took George out for a walk to the mailbox.

Two days later, while walking past the living room, George heard a guffaw. Was that *Anne* he heard?

Sure enough, there was his wife sitting on the couch, or rather rolling on the couch in convulsive laughter.

"Who's it from, dear?" George couldn't imagine what would make his wife laugh like that. She was more the gentle tittering type.

"Why, it's from you, silly." You've written a suicide note. Of all people, George. Oh, for goodness sake, you couldn't kill a rabbit, much less yourself. Were you trying to be funny? You've always had a strange sense of humor. You shouldn't be writing such stuff. Some people might take you seriously. Now go get changed. Don't you remember? Frank and Lois asked us over for dinner. Now stop frowning, George. Hurry up, we'll be late."

APPROACHING WILDERNESS

He fumbled through his knapsack, rechecking the contents, especially the two loaves of bread he had baked last night. And the fifth of Bacardi 151—the most buzz for the buck. For a brief moment he thought of the curving naked landscape of his wife, still asleep. She'd worry, of course. Then, wincing, he remembered. He saw a casket covered with her favorite daffodils. And he saw his stupid stony face, still dry. What was wrong with him? A man should cry at his wife's funeral.

But he knew Ellen would worry. That girl could worry enough for the two of them. The fact that she was divorced now and her two screwed up kids were who knows where didn't help. Or that she felt she never had much chance to get to know her old man, what with all his business trips while she was growing up. Probably never should have had her, but Sarah didn't want an abortion and that was that. And he knew the little phone Nazi would call at exactly 9:45 a.m. to check up on him, so he better call her later from the road. Grabbing his walking stick near the door, he slipped off into the pre-dawn darkness.

For a time he closed his eyes as he walked, feeling each rut and turn in the road with his feet while reaching out to touch familiar trees and boulders. Onward the road pulled him, up Juniper Ridge and down through the wash, where the night's cool air had settled. Off to his right a great horned owl hooted. A propitious sign. He hooted back and laughed.

To the east he could just see the outline of the Black Hills emerging. This was the part of the journey he loved best. It didn't matter what far off wilderness he was headed for. It was the act of setting off before dawn in the direction of his goal that filled his heart with joy. Indeed, when he finally did arrive at his destination, its reality never quite matched his initial wonder and anticipation of the unknown. Approaching wilderness was better than being there.

Not that he was much of a wilderness explorer. In his ninety plus years he had managed to actually visit some wild areas, but in reality he was more of a dreamer. Many were the trips he had made, armed only with maps and travel books, from the comfort of his easy chair. Passionately he would trace his fingers along contour lines, imagining the feel of changing topography and unfolding vistas. No need to worry about rain, blisters or black flies.

But this time only a real trip would do. Lately he could think of nothing else but wilderness—all the magical places he had never seen and never would. The Sawtooths. North Cascades. Boundary Waters. Kings Canyon. The Brooks Range. Grand Staircase-Escalante. Reciting them had always brought him comfort, a distraction from the all too orderly life he had constructed. But now they had become an aching obsession, phantoms of an untrammeled world he still longed to see.

Grimacing, he sat down on a boulder and rummaged through his knapsack. He swallowed half a dozen triple strength Glucosamine tablets and loosened his boots. It's going to be a long trip, old boy. Keep moving.

In no time he had found his stride. Once he got into the zone, he could walk for miles. Pumping his arms, he stuck out his chest, inhaling deeply. Walking was his answer to everything—hangovers, arthritis, even the loss of his wife.

His plan was simple. He needed to see real wilderness again. Maybe even a wolf or a grizzly. He needed to be out in the Wild.

But Ellen had a different plan. She had found a "nice little" assisted living center. It had won awards and was only a few miles from her house.

She would come visit every day.

"Dad, you'll love it. You won't have to worry about that smelly old cabin. You'll have a comfortable apartment and get all your meals in the dining room. You'll meet new people. Everything is planned, with trips and fun activities. They've even got a nightly poker game. You'll be happy there."

"So why don't you just go and move there yourself?"

Ellen clenched her teeth. He was trying to bait her and she knew it. She resented the little boy he had become after her mother died. There was no one left now to tame him. He was all alone in that shack, in the middle of nowhere. One day, she would find him dead on the floor. Why did she have to be the one? He didn't give a rat's ass about her or anyone. But no matter. She would not let him win, this time.

"Come on, Dad. Don't you want to be happy?"

"Not particularly. Happiness is overrated, if you ask me."

One thing about Ellen, once she gets her mind made up there's no stopping her. He had even gone to see the place, just to shut her up. He had to admit it wasn't as bad as he imagined, all shiny bright and perfect. His resistance was weakening. With each passing day, he became less sure of himself, less able to resist. He knew his solitary days at the cabin were numbered.

He still didn't know exactly where he was going, but as he walked the details fell into place as they always did. He would head northeast and keep a low profile, crossing roads only when he had to. He didn't trust his Nazi daughter. Funny, he couldn't remember when he had started calling her that. Maybe it was that clipped, severe way she had of telling him what he ought to do. Or that she always beat him down with her arguments. Why couldn't she understand that a man needs more than just security and comfortable surroundings? But surely she would come looking for him once he told her about his plan. Fortunately, there was still plenty of wild country around in which a man could hide from his daughter. He would make for the big timber, then wind through desert scrub to the Colorado, crossing at Lee's Ferry. Then follow the Paria River to wander through the endless canyons of Escalante. And from there who knows, maybe he would even make it to Yellowstone and see his first wolf.

His reverie was interrupted by a sudden obnoxious sound. Fumbling through his knapsack, he found the source of his torment—the new cell phone Ellen had bought him last week. So we can always be connected, she said. *Fuck* connections! The world is too connected, too absorbed in its own shit. Why did he ever agree to one? He opened the gadget and pressed it to his ear. "Hello. *Hello.*" He pressed a button, then another. "*Hello, goddamnit!*" It started beeping as if about to explode. He threw it far and long. The sun was just coming up as he turned from the road and headed into the scrub.

For a while he followed the ridgeline past the Indian ruins. In both directions he could see throngs of new houses and cabins advancing like locusts across the valleys and up the once unsullied slopes. Generations of new retirees and refugees from California and other big government states looking to get away from it all. Pretty soon the ridge would be nothing but an endless line of houses and condos. He was glad he would not live to see it.

Descending from the ridge, he paused at the edge of a narrow wash. From the look of the pinyon-juniper country he knew he was somewhere in the national forest. Coffee would be nice, but he was too keyed up to build a fire. He washed down his breakfast bar with a few slugs of water and resumed walking.

The winding path of the wash wasn't the most direct way north, but it perfectly suited his mood. He had been planning this trip for years. What was the rush? He knew the state highway lay just a few miles to the east and the wash wasn't exactly wilderness. But for him it had a wild feel, as if he were the first to explore it. Ignoring a startled scrub-jay, he squeezed through the underbrush and clambered over the rocks with boyish glee.

He flopped down for a minute to catch his breath, admiring the patchwork of sun-dappled colors on the rocks and leaves. No awe-inspiring vista, but it would do. He took off his boots and rubbed his throbbing feet. Though he had walked past the pain for a while, it was back. He knew his arthritis would make him pay dearly for this trip. It was in all his joints now. He could feel them grinding away and disintegrating like the life he had once had. Maybe someday he would do as his doctor and Ellen suggested and have them all replaced. Then he could become the Bionic Man. There would be no more pain, no more startling jabs to remind him of the bittersweet beauty of life and death. O.K., feet, let's go. One more time for the old man.

His brain swirled. Walking always stimulated him, but this time his thoughts came at him like a flashflood. Childhood memories of family trips to the Smokies and White Mountains came jumbled with fears of falling through the ice alone on a remote Michigan pond and lusty encounters with Sarah beneath a leaky tent in the Everglades. The day when Ellen was born, all thought of abortion forgotten. And the day when Sarah's lab test came back and the world died.

And he thought of another day when he first started losing words. It wasn't just temporarily being unable to find the right word but forgetting it completely. Like looking at water and not knowing what to call it. He would be reading the newspaper and suddenly come to a dead stop at a word that looked vaguely familiar but unknown. Looking it up in the dictionary would only add to his unease, as if it were a word he had never learned.

He thought of Sarah and how she would have hated losing even a simple verb. For him losing an occasional word now and again was more inconvenient than disturbing. After all, he still had thousands left inside him. It's no big deal. But Sarah would have been horrified. For her words were everything. Fortunately she was sharp right till the end. He could think of few advantages to dying before your time, but maybe this was one.

He slowed his pace, as if trying at the same time to slow his thoughts. Breathing deeply, he started to remember something from this morning, something he was supposed to do. He checked off the things he had done. Turn off the stove. Shake the toilet handle. Lock the door. Then what? It probably wasn't important. That had become his mantra lately in response to all the little nagging feelings of forgetfulness. A man shouldn't have to remember every fucking thing.

Approaching Wilderness

Just getting up in the morning is hard enough. Who cares what day it is? They're all alike, coming one right after the other whether you're ready for them or not.

He left the wash and trudged up the next ridge to get his bearings. Wheezing, he slumped on a boulder and shook his head. What a pathetic old geezer. But at the sight of the Coconino Plateau, he quickly forgot his pains. He was a boy again, on a trip to Grand Canyon, where he had his first vision of a wilder world beyond the guardrail. He could feel himself falling into the multi-colored layers below as the canyon walls closed around him. It was the same feeling he always had when he hiked down into the canyon. It was like walking back into the earth's womb when life was still emerging and all things were possible.

After a quick lunch of cheese and fruit, he lay back and let the sun soak into his joints. It was already past noon and he still had a lot of ground to cover. He watched as a collared lizard bobbed its head from a nearby rock. He bobbed his head back. Even without words there were still ways to communicate, though he wasn't sure exactly what was being said. The lizard bobbed its head again.

He headed down the ridge toward the distant forest-carpeted plateau. For the most part he kept to the trees, following whatever shade he could find in the open woodlands. Occasionally he would hastily cross a gravel road where the spell was temporarily broken. He was resting more frequently now and for longer periods. He couldn't remember when he had last walked so far. He leaned back against a big pinyon. The shade felt good in the hot summer afternoon. It wouldn't hurt to rest a while longer.

When he awoke the tree's long shadow told him he had slept too long. Only a couple of hours remained till nightfall. He had hoped to make it at least to the interstate, but he knew it was still far off. He set off again at a brisk pace, cursing his old body. For a while he managed to keep it up until he tripped over a log and fell on his bad knee. Slowly he got up, cursing yet another offending joint that had let him down. Leaning heavily on his walking stick he hobbled on, feeling stupid and alone.

He decided to make camp in an outcrop of lichen-crusted granite that rose like a castle from a grove of venerable oak trees. There was a nice private wedge between the rocks, filled with oak duff, where he could bed down for the night. Plenty of dead branches were nearby and in no time at all he had built himself a competent campfire. Building a good fire had always been proof of his manhood. At least there was one thing he could still do.

He cleared a flat rock and laid out his dinner.

He opened a can of split pea soup and set it upon some coals. Then he cut a slice of bread and a wedge of cheese. He had plenty of trail mix and beef jerky, enough to last for days. He was certainly better off than John Muir, who often explored the High Sierras with little more than some tea and flour. What more does a man need?

Then he remembered the rum. By his third drink his memories were well lubricated. Stirring the fire, he thought back to a camping trip in the Smokies. Just out of college, with his two hippie friends, he recalled the camaraderie of that moment—three outlaw rebels against the war, the Establishment, tradition, and anything old—hiding out in the wilderness. But mostly he remembered the drinking and pot smoking around the campfire. Then stumbling up to their sleeping bags on the bear platform and talking each other to sleep with philosophical bullshit.

He awoke four hours later with a jolt. The booze had mostly worn off, and he had become suddenly aware of a sharp rock projecting against his spine. Now he remembered why he hadn't camped again since his twenties. Shivering, he pulled his blanket tighter around him. Dawn was still a long way off. He could feel every joint screaming at him. What was he doing here? He stood up and stared at the stars. But the stars that had always fascinated him were now just alien points of light. He didn't have a clue where he was.

He built up the fire, stoking the flames ever higher as if to make his memories burn brighter again. But all he could remember was something about heading northeast and the sound of a cell phone smashing.

He made instant coffee, then gulped down a breakfast of trail mix, aspirin and glucosamine. Rising stiffly, he spread apart the fire's ashes and pissed on them with a painful, erratic stream. His knee was still bothering him from the fall. But he knew he had to keep walking. He turned to the northeast.

After a few hours, he was no closer to an answer. At least for the time being he had largely moved past the pain. His rest stops and naps were getting much longer. When had he become such a wimp? There were days when he could walk twenty miles and more, or so he thought. He hated the hobbling old man he had become. But most of all, he hated not being able to remember.

It was late afternoon when he came to the interstate. For a long interval, he stared helplessly across the wide expanse, relentlessly flowing with the Friday traffic of northbound city dwellers heading for the high country. He saw it as a great river blocking his way, the antithesis of whatever it was he was seeking. He took a deep breath and made a run for it. A blue Hummer doing ninety just narrowly missed him as its owner flipped him the bird. Struggling to higher ground, he grabbed the trunk of a ponderosa pine and hugged it. And he thought of his wife. Sarah, where are you? Please forgive me. And for the first time in years he cried.

The setting sun felt good on his back as he headed upslope through the tall trees. After several miles he came to an old forest road with few signs of recent use. It was headed in the right direction, so he readily acceded to its linear command.

As he passed over a brook, he paused to admire the intricate handiwork of the stone bridge. It seemed out of place in this world, a testament to a distant age when workmanship still mattered. Obviously the work of Civilian Conservation Corps elves, he mused, that legendary race of craftsmen who forged wonders out of native stone and timber while helping to rebuild a battered country.

Suddenly three sullen riders on ATV's roared past him, nearly knocking him over. He looked down the road in disgust. There are no answers here, old boy, and you know it. All this will lead to is another road. Off to his right he noticed a steep canyon running up a nearby slope, its sharp rocky mouth entreating him to climb up and explore its hidden corners.

With newfound confidence, he turned away from the road and followed the creek as it trickled up the mountainside. He clambered around huge boulders through tangles of wild grape vines and thorn bush that tore at his face and clothes. He was far into the canyon now, beyond all that was safe and secure. There would be no one to know he was up there, no one to know he was gone. But then he saw a face. *Ellen!* How did she find him? He would not go back. He must keep going. But he was getting weaker. Just need to rest a while. He leaned against a rock and gazed up the canyon. He could see wonders ahead—the fabled canyons of Escalante. Wonders at the heart of the world. He closed his eyes and dreamed.

****

The hospice was bright and clean, with a perfect view of the San Francisco Peaks. Ellen had taken him there after the last stroke. Neighbors had found him lying unconscious just a few hundred yards down the road from his cabin. She sat at his bedside, hoping as always for some little sign of recognition. But she knew there would be none. She stared at the face of the father she barely knew. Come on, Dad, give me something, anything. But it was just that same old stupid stony face. He opened his eyes, staring not at her but at somewhere in the distance, at the last wild empty places. Then he smiled and bowed his head.

Ellen closed his eyes. She wanted to cry but couldn't. Well, at least you gave me that much, old man. You finally made it to the wild. You're home now.

ABOUT THE AUTHOR

Gene Twaronite's short stories, poems, and essays have appeared in numerous literary journals and magazines. He is the author of the middle grade novel *The Family That Wasn't* and the young adult novel *My Vacation in Hell*, as well as a collection of his children's stories *Dragon Daily News: Stories of Imagination for Children of All Ages*. Follow more of his writing at his blog "The Twaronite Zone." www.thetwaronitezone.com

Printed in Great Britain
by Amazon